D1737897

Shark

amicus readers 2

by Wendy Perkins

Say hello to amicus readers.

amicus readers

You'll find our helpful dog, Amicus, chasing a ball—to let you know the reading level of a book.

A
Learn to Read
Frequent repetition of sentence structures, high frequency words, and familiar topics provide ample support for brand new readers. Approximately 100 words.

1
Read Independently
Repetition is mixed with varied sentence structures and 6 to 8 content words per book are introduced with photo label and picture glossary supports. Approximately 150 words.

2
Read to Know More
These books feature a higher text load with additional nonfiction features such as more photos, time lines, and text divided into sections. Approximately 250 words.

Amicus Readers are published by Amicus
P.O. Box 1329, Mankato, Minnesota 56002

Series Editor   Rebecca Glaser
Series Designer   Heather Dreisbach
Photo Researcher   Heather Dreisbach

Printed in the United States of America at Corporate Graphics in North Mankato, Minnesota.

1023
3-2011

10 9 8 7 6 5 4 3 2 1

Library of Congress Cataloging-in-Publication Data
Perkins, Wendy, 1957-
    Shark / by Wendy Perkins.
        p. cm. – (Amicus Readers. Animal life cycles)
    Includes index.
    Summary: "Presents the life cycle of a shark from mating and birth to adult. Includes time line of life cycle and sequencing activity" –Provided by publisher.
    ISBN 978-1-60753-154-8 (library binding)
    1. Sharks–Life cycles–Juvenile literature. I. Title.
    QL638.9.P434 2012
    597.3–dc22
                                    2010035672

Table of Contents

A Life Cycle

Swish, swish! An adult shark sweeps its tail back and forth as it swims through a school of sharks. They have gathered to breed. It is part of their life cycle.

pup

breeding

adult

juvenile

5

Breeding

During breeding, a male shark fertilizes the eggs inside a female. A female shark breeds with many males, then leaves. The male sharks do not help raise the young.

Some types of sharks lay eggs on rocks or seaweed. But most kinds of sharks give birth to live young. Their babies, called pups, grow inside the female's body.

▶ shark egg

pregnant
shark

Pups

Nine months to one year after breeding, the female gives birth to pups in a group called a litter. There may be as many as 15 pups in a litter. The female swims away after she gives birth.

Breeding

Pups born
9 to 12 months
after breeding

Each pup takes care of itself and hunts its own food. Bigger sharks and other large fish eat shark pups. The pups stay in shallow water where they are safer.

Juvenile

After a couple of years, the pup has grown into a juvenile shark. It is big enough to hunt in deeper water where there are large fish to eat.

Breeding ——— Pups born 9 to 12 months after breeding

Juvenile shark
2 years old

Adult

It takes many years before the shark becomes an adult that can breed. How long it takes depends on the kind of shark it is. A great white shark can breed when it is between 10 and 15 years old.

Breeding

Pups born
9 to 12 months
after breeding

Juvenile shark
2 years old

Adult shark
10 to 15
years old

Even after it is an adult, the shark can grow bigger. It keeps growing slowly throughout its life. Sharks can live about thirty years.

Juvenile shark
2 years old

Adult shark
10 to 15
years old

Photo Glossary

breed
when a male and female join together to make babies

juvenile
the stage of life between a pup and adult shark

life cycle
the stages of an animal's life from birth to death

litter
a group of shark pups born at the same time

pup
the name for a baby shark

school
the name for a group of fish that live together

Life Cycle Puzzle

The stages of a shark's life are all mixed up.
Can you put them in the right order?

pup

breeding

adult

juvenile

Ideas for Teachers and Parents

Children are fascinated by animals, and even more so by life cycles as they grow up themselves. *Animal Life Cycles,* an Amicus Readers level 2 series, lets kids compare life stages of animals. The books use labels and a photo glossary to introduce new vocabulary. The activity page and time lines reinforce sequencing skills.

Before Reading

- Ask the children to tell what they know about sharks or shark babies.
- Have the students talk about whether they've seen sharks.
- Look at the photo glossary words. Tell children to watch for them as they read the book.

Read the Book

- "Walk" through the book and look at the photos. Point out the time line showing how long sharks spend at each stage.
- Ask the students to read the book independently.
- Provide support where necessary. Show students how the highlighted words are explained in the photo glossary.

After Reading

- Have students do the activity on page 22 and put the stages of the shark life cycle in order.
- Compare the life cycle of a shark with other animals in the series. *Does it have the same number of stages?*
- Have the students compare the human life cycle to a shark's life cycle. *How is it different? How is it the same?*

Index

Web Sites

All About Sharks: Enchanted Learning
http://www.enchantedlearning.com/subjects/sharks/

Great White Shark: National Geographic Kids
http://kids.nationalgeographic.com/kids/animals/
creaturefeature/great-white-shark/

Sharks: Kid Zone
http://www.kidzone.ws/sharks/